HORRID HENRY
AND THE
ABOMINABLE
SNOWMAN

Francesca Simon spent her childhood on the beach
in California, and then went to Yale and Oxford
Universities to study medieval history and literature.
She now lives in London with her family. She has
written over 50 books and won the Children's Book
of the Year in 2008 at the Galaxy British Book Awards
for *Horrid Henry and the Abominable Snowman*.

HORRiD HENRY BOOKS

HORRiD HENRY
AND THE
ABOMiNABLE
SNOWMAN

Francesca Simon
Illustrated by Tony Ross

Orion
Children's Books

ORION CHILDREN'S BOOKS

First published in Great Britain in 2007 by Orion Children's Books
This edition published in 2016 by Hodder and Stoughton

6

Text copyright © Francesca Simon, 2007
Illustrations copyright © Tony Ross, 2007

The moral rights of the author and illustrator have been asserted.

A CIP catalogue record for this book
is available from the British Library.

ISBN 978 1 4072 3042 9

Printed and bound in Great Britain
by Clays Ltd, St Ives plc

The paper and board used in this book are
made from wood from responsible sources.

MIX
Paper from
responsible sources
FSC® C104740

Orion Children's Books
An imprint of
Hachette Children's Group
Part of Hodder and Stoughton
Carmelite House
50 Victoria Embankment
London EC4Y 0DZ

An Hachette UK Company
www.hachette.co.uk

www.hachettechildrens.co.uk

For my niece, Ava Rose

CONTENTS

1

HORRID HENRY
AND THE
ABOMINABLE SNOWMAN

Moody Margaret took aim.

Thwack!

A snowball whizzed past and smacked Sour Susan in the face.

'AAAAARRGGHHH!' shrieked Susan.

'Ha ha, got you,' said Margaret.

'You big meanie,' howled Susan, scooping up a fistful of snow and hurling it at Margaret.

Thwack!

Susan's snowball smacked Moody Margaret in the face.

'OWWWW!' screamed Margaret.

'You've blinded me.'

'Good!' screamed Susan.

'I hate you!' shouted Margaret, shoving Susan.

'I hate you more!' shouted Susan, pushing Margaret.

Splat! Margaret toppled into the snow.

Splat! Susan toppled into the snow.

'I'm going home to build my own snowman,' sobbed Susan.

'Fine. I'll win without you,' said Margaret.

'Won't!'

'Will! I'm going to win, copycat,' shrieked Margaret.

'*I'm* going to win,' shrieked Susan. 'I kept my best ideas secret.'

'Win? Win what?' demanded Horrid Henry, stomping down his front steps in his snow boots and swaggering over. Henry could hear the word *win* from miles away.

'Haven't you heard about the competition?' said Sour Susan. 'The prize is—'

'Shut up! Don't tell him,' shouted Moody Margaret, packing snow onto her snowman's head.

Win? Competition? Prize? Horrid Henry's ears quivered. What secret were they trying to keep from him? Well, not for long. Horrid Henry was an expert at extracting information.

3

'Oh, the competition. I know all about *that*,' lied Horrid Henry. 'Hey, great snowman,' he added, strolling casually over to Margaret's snowman and pretending to admire her work.

Now, what should he do? Torture? Margaret's ponytail was always a tempting target. And snow down her jumper would make her talk.

What about blackmail? He could spread some great rumours about Margaret at school. Or . . .

'Tell me about the competition or the ice guy gets it,' said Horrid Henry suddenly, leaping over to the snowman and putting his hands round its neck.

'You wouldn't dare,' gasped Moody Margaret.

Henry's mittened hands got ready to push.

'Bye bye, head,' hissed Horrid Henry. 'Nice knowing you.'

Margaret's snowman wobbled.

'Stop!' screamed Margaret. 'I'll tell you. It doesn't matter 'cause you'll never ever win.'

'Keep talking,' said Horrid Henry warily, watching out in case Susan tried to ambush him from behind.

'Frosty Freeze are having a best snowman competition,' said Moody Margaret, glaring. 'The winner gets a year's free supply of ice cream. The judges will decide tomorrow morning.

Now get away from my snowman.'

Horrid Henry walked off in a daze, his jaw dropping. Margaret and Susan pelted him with snowballs but Henry didn't even notice. Free ice cream for a year direct from the Frosty Freeze Ice Cream factory. Oh wow! Horrid Henry couldn't believe it. Mum and Dad were so mean and horrible they hardly ever let him have ice cream. And when they did, they never *ever* let him put on his own hot fudge sauce and whipped cream and sprinkles. Or even scoop the ice cream himself. Oh no.

Well, when he won the Best Snowman Competition they couldn't stop him gorging on Chunky Chocolate Fab Fudge Caramel Delight, or Vanilla Whip Tutti-Fruitti Toffee Treat. Oh boy! Henry could taste that glorious ice cream now. He'd live on ice cream. He'd bathe in ice cream. He'd sleep in ice cream. Everyone from school would turn up at his house when the Frosty Freeze truck arrived bringing his weekly barrels. No matter how much they begged, Horrid Henry would send them all away. No way was he sharing a drop of his precious ice cream with *anyone*.

And all he had to do was to build the best snowman in the neighbourhood. Pah! Henry's was sure to be the winner. He would build the biggest snowman of all. And not just a snowman. A snowman with claws, and horns, and fangs. A vampire-demon-monster snowman. An Abominable Snowman. Yes!

7

Henry watched Margaret and
Susan rolling snow and packing their
saggy snowman. Ha. Snow heap, more
like.

'You'll never win with *that*,' jeered
Horrid Henry. 'Your snowman is
pathetic.'

'Better than yours,' snapped Margaret.

Horrid Henry rolled his eyes.

'Obviously, because I haven't started mine yet.'

'We've got a big head start on you, so ha ha ha,' said Susan. 'We're building a ballerina snowgirl.'

'Shut up, Susan,' screamed Margaret.

A ballerina snowgirl? What a stupid idea. If that was the best they could do Henry was sure to win.

'Mine will be the biggest, the best, the most gigantic snowman ever seen,' said Horrid Henry. 'And much better than your stupid snow dwarf.'

'Fat chance,' sneered Margaret.

'Yeah, Henry,' sneered Susan. 'Ours is the best.'

'No way,' said Horrid Henry, starting to roll a gigantic ball of snow for Abominable's big belly. There was no time to lose.

Up the path, down the path, across the garden, down the side, back and forth, back and forth, Horrid Henry rolled the biggest ball of snow ever seen.

'Henry, can I build a snowman with you?' came a little voice.

'No,' said Henry, starting to carve out some clawed feet.

'Oh please,' said Peter. 'We could build a great big one together. Like a bunny snowman, or a—'

'No!' said Henry. 'It's *my* snowman. Build your own.'

'Muuuummmm!' wailed Peter. 'Henry won't let me build a snowman with him.'

'Don't be horrid, Henry,' said Mum. 'Why don't you build one together?'

'NO!!!' said Horrid Henry. He wanted to make his *own* snowman.

If he built a snowman with his stupid worm brother, he'd have to share the prize. Well, no way. He wanted all that

11

ice cream for himself. And his Abominable Snowman was sure to be the best. Why share a prize when you didn't have to?

'Get away from my snowman, Peter,' hissed Henry.

Perfect Peter snivelled. Then he started to roll a tiny ball of snow.

'And get your own snow,' said Henry. 'All this is mine.'

'Muuuuuum!' wailed Peter. 'Henry's hogging all the snow.'

★

'We're done,' trilled Moody Margaret. 'Beat *this* if you can.'

Horrid Henry looked at Margaret and Susan's snowgirl, complete with a big pink tutu wound round the waist. It was as big as Margaret.

'That old heap of snow is nothing compared to *mine*,' bragged Horrid Henry.

Moody Margaret and Sour Susan looked at Henry's Abominable Snowman, complete with Viking horned helmet, fangs, and hairy scary claws. It was a few centimetres taller than Henry.

'Nah nah ne nah nah, mine's bigger,' boasted Henry.

'Nah nah ne nah nah, mine's better,' boasted Margaret.

'How do you like *my* snowman?' said Peter. 'Do you think *I* could win?'

Horrid Henry stared at Perfect Peter's tiny snowman. It didn't even have a head, just a long, thin, lumpy body with two stones stuck in the top for eyes.

Horrid Henry howled with laughter.

'That's the worst snowman I've ever seen,' said Henry. 'It doesn't even have a head. That's a snow carrot.'

'It is not,' wailed Peter. 'It's a big bunny.'

'Henry! Peter! Suppertime,' called Mum.

Henry stuck out his tongue at Margaret.

'And don't you dare touch my snowman.'

Margaret stuck out her tongue at Henry.

'And don't you dare touch *my* snowgirl.'

'I'll be watching you, Margaret.'

'I'll be watching *you*, Henry.'

They glared at each other.

Henry woke.

What was that noise? Was Margaret sabotaging his snowman? Was Susan stealing his snow?

Horrid Henry dashed to the window.

Phew. There was his Abominable Snowman, big as ever, dwarfing every other snowman in the street. Henry's was definitely the biggest, and the best. Umm boy, he could taste that Triple Fudge Gooey Chocolate Chip Peanut Butter Marshmallow Custard ice cream right now.

Horrid Henry climbed back into bed.

A tiny doubt nagged him.

Was his snowman *definitely* bigger than Margaret's?

'Course it was, thought Henry.

'Are you sure?' rumbled his tummy.

'Yeah,' said Henry.

'Because I really want that ice cream,' growled his tummy. 'Why don't you double-check?'

Horrid Henry got out of bed.

He was sure his was bigger and better than Margaret's. He was absolutely sure his was bigger and better.

But what if—

I can't sleep without checking, thought Henry.

Tip toe.

Tip toe.

Tip toe.

Horrid Henry slipped out of the front door.

The whole street was silent and white and frosty. Every house had a snowman in front. All of them much smaller than Henry's, he noted with satisfaction.

And there was his Abominable Snowman looming up, Viking horns scraping the sky. Horrid Henry gazed at him proudly. Next to him was Peter's pathetic pimple, with its stupid black stones. A snow lump, thought Henry.

Then he looked over at Margaret's
snowgirl. Maybe it had fallen down,
thought Henry hopefully. And if it hadn't
maybe he could help it on its way ...

He looked again. And again. That evil
fiend!

Margaret had sneaked an extra ball of
snow on top, complete with a huge
flowery hat.

19

That little cheater, thought Horrid Henry indignantly. She'd sneaked out after bedtime and made hers bigger than his. How dare she? Well, he'd fix Margaret. He'd add more snow to his right away.

Horrid Henry looked around. Where could he find more snow? He'd already used up every drop on his front lawn to build his giant, and no new snow had fallen.

Henry shivered.

Brr, it was freezing. He needed more snow, and he needed it fast. His slippers were starting to feel very wet and cold.

Horrid Henry eyed Peter's pathetic lump of snow. Hmmn, thought Horrid Henry.

Hmmn, thought Horrid Henry again. Well, it's not doing any good sitting

21

there, thought Henry. Someone could trip over it. Someone could hurt themselves. In fact, Peter's snowlump was a danger. He had to act fast before someone fell over it and broke a leg.

Quickly, he scooped up Peter's

snowman and stacked it carefully on top of his. Then standing on his tippy toes, he balanced the Abominable Snowman's Viking horns on top.

Da dum!

Much better. And *much* bigger than Margaret's.

Teeth chattering, Horrid Henry sneaked back into his house and crept into bed. Ice cream, here I come, thought Horrid Henry.

Ding dong.

Horrid Henry jumped out of bed. What a morning to oversleep.

Perfect Peter ran and opened the door.

'We're from the Frosty Freeze Ice Cream Factory,' said the man, beaming. 'And you've got the winning snowman out front.'

'I won!' screeched Horrid Henry. 'I won!' He tore down the stairs and out

the door. Oh what a lovely lovely day.
The sky was blue. The sun was shining
— huh???

Horrid Henry looked around.

Horrid Henry's Abominable Snowman
was gone.

'Margaret!' screamed Henry. 'I'll kill
you!'

But Moody Margaret's snowgirl was
gone, too.

The Abominable Snowman's helmet lay
on its side on the ground. All that was
left of Henry's snowman was . . . Peter's
pimple, with its two black stone eyes. A
big blue ribbon was pinned to the top.

'But that's *my* snowman,' said Perfect Peter.

'But . . . but . . .' said Horrid Henry.

'You mean, *I* won?' said Peter.

'That's wonderful, Peter,' said Mum.

'That's fantastic, Peter,' said Dad.

'All the others melted,' said the Frosty Freeze man. 'Yours was the only one left. It must have been a giant.'

'It was,' howled Horrid Henry.

2

HORRID HENRY'S RAINY DAY

Horrid Henry was bored. Horrid Henry was fed up. He'd been banned from the computer for rampaging through Our Town Museum. He'd been banned from watching TV just because he was caught watching a *teeny* tiny bit extra after he'd been told to switch it off straight after Mutant Max. Could he help it if an exciting new series about a rebel robot had started right after? How would he know if it were any good unless he watched some of it?

It was completely unfair and all Peter's fault for telling on him, and Mum and

Dad were the meanest, most horrible parents in the world.

And now he was stuck indoors, all day long, with absolutely nothing to do.

The rain splattered down. The house was grey. The world was grey. The universe was grey.

'I'm bored!' wailed Horrid Henry.

'Read a book,' said Mum.

'Do your homework,' said Dad.

'NO!' said Horrid Henry.

'Then tidy your room,' said Mum.

'Unload the dishwasher,' said Dad.

'Empty the bins,' said Mum.

'NO WAY!' shrieked Horrid Henry. What was he, a slave? Better keep out of his parents' way, or they'd come up with even more horrible things for him to do.

Horrid Henry stomped up to his boring bedroom and slammed the door. Uggh. He hated all his toys. He hated all his music. He hated all his games.

UGGGHHHHHH! What could he do?

Aha.

He could always check to see what Peter was up to.

Perfect Peter was sitting in his room arranging stamps in his stamp album.

'Peter is a baby, Peter is a baby,' jeered Horrid Henry, sticking his head round the door.

'Don't call me baby,' said Perfect Peter.

'OK, Duke of Poop,' said Henry.

'Don't call me Duke!' shrieked Peter.

'OK, Poopsicle,' said Henry.

'MUUUUM!' wailed Peter. 'Henry called me Poopsicle!'

'Don't be horrid, Henry!' shouted Mum. 'Stop calling your brother names.'

Horrid Henry smiled sweetly at Peter.

'OK, Peter, 'cause I'm so nice, I'll let you make a list of ten names that you don't want to be called,' said Henry. 'And it will only cost you £1.'

£1! Perfect Peter could not believe his ears. Peter would pay much more than that never to be called Poopsicle again.

'Is this a trick, Henry?' said Peter.

'No,' said Henry. 'How dare you? I make you a good offer, and you accuse me. Well, just for that—'

'Wait,' said Peter. 'I accept.' He handed Henry a pound coin. At last, all those horrid names would be banned. Henry would never call him Duke of Poop again.

Peter got out a piece of paper and a pencil.

Now, let's see, what to put on the list, thought Peter. Poopsicle, for a start. And I hate being called Baby, and Nappy Face, and Duke of Poop. Peter wrote and wrote and wrote.

'OK, Henry, here's the list,' said Peter.

NAMES I DON'T WANT
TO BE CALLED

1. Poopsicle
2. Duke of Poop
3. Ugly
4. Nappyface
5. Baby
6 Toad
7. Smelly Toad
8. Ugg
9. Worm
10. Wibble pants

Horrid Henry scanned the list. 'Fine, pongy pants,' said Henry. 'Sorry, I meant poopy pants. Or was it smelly nappy?'

'MUUUMM!' wailed Peter. 'Henry's calling me names!'

'Henry!' screamed Mum. 'For the last time, can't you leave your brother alone?'

Horrid Henry
considered. *Could*
he leave that
worm alone?

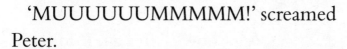

'Peter is a
frog, Peter is a
frog,' chanted Henry.

'MUUUUUUMMMMM!' screamed
Peter.

'That's it, Henry!' shouted Mum. 'No
pocket money for a week. Go to your
room and stay there.'

'Fine!' shrieked Henry. 'You'll all be
sorry when I'm dead.' He stomped down
the hall and slammed his bedroom door
as hard as he could. *Why* were his parents
so mean and horrible? He was hardly
bothering Peter at all. Peter *was* a frog.
Henry was only telling the truth.

Boy would they be sorry when he'd
died of boredom stuck up here.

If only we'd let him watch a little extra

TV, Mum would wail. Would
that have been so terrible?

If only we hadn't made
him do any chores, Dad
would sob.

Why didn't
I let Henry call
me names, Peter would
howl. After all, I do have
smelly pants.

And now
it's too late and we're
sooooooo sorry, they
would shriek.

But wait. *Would* they be
sorry? Peter would grab his room. And
all his best toys. His arch enemy Stuck-
Up Steve could come over and snatch
anything he wanted, even his skeleton
bank and Goo-Shooter. Peter could
invade the Purple Hand fort and Henry
couldn't stop him. Moody Margaret

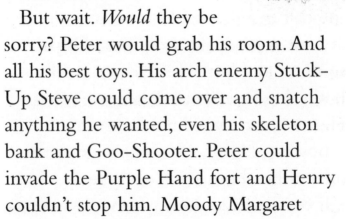

could hop over the wall and nick his flag. And his biscuits. And his Dungeon Drink Kit. Even his ... Supersoaker.

NOOOOOO!!!

Horrid Henry went pale. He had to stop those rapacious thieves. But how?

I could come back and haunt them, thought Horrid Henry. Yes! That would teach those grave-robbers not to mess with me.

'OOOOOOO, get out of my rooooooooooom, you horrrrrrible toooooooooooad,' he would moan at Peter.

'Touch my Gooooooo-shoooooter and you'll be morphed into ectoplasm,' he'd groan spookily from under Stuck-Up Steve's bed. Ha! That would show him.

Or he'd pop out from inside Moody Margaret's wardrobe.

'Giiiiive Henrrrrry's toyyyys back, you mis-er-a-ble sliiiiiimy snake,' he would rasp. That would teach her a thing or two.

Henry smiled. But fun as it would be to haunt people, he'd rather stop horrible

enemies snatching his stuff in the first place.

And then suddenly Horrid Henry had a brilliant, spectacular idea. Hadn't Mum told him just the other day that people wrote wills to say who they wanted to get all their stuff when they died? Henry had been thrilled.

'So when you die I get all your money!' Henry beamed. Wow. The house would be his! And the car! And he'd be boss of the TV, 'cause it would be his, too!!! And the only shame was—

'Couldn't you just give it all to me now?' asked Henry.

'Henry!' snapped Mum. 'Don't be horrid.'

There was no time to lose. He had to write a will immediately.

Horrid Henry sat down at his desk and grabbed some paper.

MY WILL
WARNING: DO NOT READ UNLESS
I AM DEAD!!!! I mean it!!!!

If you're reading this it's because I'm dead and you aren't. I wish you were dead and I wasn't, so I could have all *your* stuff. It's so not fair.

First of all, to anyone thinking of snatching my stuff just 'cause I'm dead ... BEWARE! Anyone who doesn't do what I say will get haunted by a bloodless and boneless ghoul, namely me. So there.

Now the hard bit, thought Horrid Henry. Who should get his things? Was anyone deserving enough?

Peter, you are a worm. And a toad. And an ugly baby nappy face smelly ugg wibble pants poopsicle. I leave you . . . hmmmn.

That toad really shouldn't get anything. But Peter was his brother after all. **I leave you my sweet wrappers. And a muddy twig.**

That was more than Peter deserved.

Still . . .

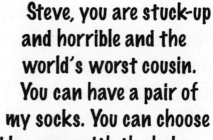

Steve, you are stuck-up and horrible and the world's worst cousin. You can have a pair of my socks. You can choose the blue ones with the holes or the falling down orange ones.

Margaret, you nit-face. I give you the Purple Hand flag to remember me by— NOT! You can have two radishes and the knight

with the chopped-off head. And
keep your paws off my
Grisly Grub Box!!! Or
else...

Miss Battle-Axe,
you are my worst
teacher ever. I leave
you a broken pencil.

Aunt Ruby, you
can have
the lime green cardigan
back that you gave me
for Christmas.

Hmmm. So far he
wasn't doing so well giving
away any of his good things.

Ralph, you can have my Goo-Shooter, but
ONLY if you give *me* your football and your
bike and your computer game Slime Ghouls.

That was more like it. After all, why
should *he* be the only one writing a will?

It was certainly a lot more fun thinking about *getting* stuff from other people than giving away his own treasures.

In fact, wouldn't he be better off helping others by telling them what he wanted? Wouldn't it be awful if Rich Aunt Ruby left him some of Steve's old clothes in her will thinking that he would be delighted? Better write to her at once.

> Dear Aunt Ruby
> I am leeving you
> Something ~~get REELY~~
> ~~GREAT~~ REELY
> REELY GREAT in
> my will, so make sure
> you leeve me loads of
> Cash in yours.
>   Your favorite nephew
>   Henry

Now, Steve. Henry was leaving him an old pair of holey socks. But Steve didn't have to *know* that, did he. For all Henry knew, Steve *loved* holey socks.

Dear Steve

You know your new
blue racing bike
with the silver trim?
Well when your dead
it wont be any use to you,
So please leave it to me
in your will
　　　　Your favourite cousin
P.S　　　　　Henry
By the way,
no need to wait till your dead,
you can give it to me now.

Right, Mum and Dad. When they were in the old people's home they'd hardly

need a thing. A rocking chair and blanket each would do fine for them.

So, how would Dad's music system look in his bedroom? And where could he put Mum's clock radio? Henry had always liked the chiming clock on their mantelpiece and the picture of the blackbird. Better go and check to see where he could put them.

Henry went into Mum and Dad's room, and grabbed an armload of stuff.

He staggered to his bedroom and dumped everything on the floor, then went back for a second helping.

Stumbling and staggering under his heavy burden, Horrid Henry swayed down the hall and crashed into Dad.

'What are you doing?' said Dad, staring. 'That's mine.'

'And those are mine,' said Mum.

'What is going on?' shrieked Mum and Dad.

'I was just checking how all this stuff will look in my room when you're in the old people's home,' said Horrid Henry.

'I'm not there yet,' said Mum.

'Put everything back,' said Dad.

Horrid Henry scowled. Here he was, just trying to think ahead, and he gets told off.

'Well, just for that I won't leave you any of my knights in my will,' said Henry.

Honestly, some people were so selfish.

3

MOODY MARGARET'S MAKEOVER

'Watch out, Gurinder! You're smearing your nail varnish,' screeched Moody Margaret. 'Violet! Don't touch your face – you're spoiling all my hard work. Susan! Sit still.'

'I am sitting still,' said Sour Susan. 'Stop pulling my hair.'

'I'm not pulling your hair,' hissed Margaret. 'I'm styling it.'

'Ouch!' squealed Susan. 'You're hurting me.'

'I am not, crybaby.'

'I'm not a crybaby,' howled Susan.

Moody Margaret sighed loudly.

'Not everyone can be naturally beautiful like me. Some people'– she glared at Susan – 'have to work at it.'

'You're not beautiful,' said Sour Susan, snorting.

'I am too,' said Margaret, preening herself.

'Are not,' said Susan. 'On the ugly scale of 1 to 10, with 1 being the ugliest, wartiest, toad, you're a 2.'

'Huh!' said Margaret. 'Well, *you're* so ugly you're minus 1. They don't have an ugly enough scale for *you*.'

'I want my money back!' shrieked Susan.

'No way!' shrieked Margaret. 'Now sit down and shut up.'

Across the wall in the next garden, deep inside the branches hiding the top secret entrance of the Purple Hand fort, a master spy pricked up his ears.

Money? Had he heard the word *money*?

What was going on next door?

Horrid Henry zipped out of his fort and dashed to the low wall separating his garden from Margaret's. Then he stared. And stared some more. He'd seen many weird things in his life. But nothing as weird as this.

Moody Margaret, Sour Susan, Lazy Linda, Vain Violet and Gorgeous Gurinder were sitting in Margaret's garden. Susan had rollers tangling her pink hair. Violet had blue mascara all over her face. Linda was covered in gold glitter. There was spilt nail varnish, face powder, and broken lipstick all over Margaret's patio.

Horrid Henry burst out laughing.

'Are you playing clowns?' said Henry.

'Huh, that's how much *you* know, Henry,' said Margaret. '*I'm* doing makeovers.'

'What's that?' said Henry.

'It's when you change how people look, dummy,' said Margaret.

'I knew that,' lied Henry. 'I just wanted to see if you did.'

Margaret waved a leaflet in his face.

MARGARET'S

MAGNIFICENT MAKEOVERS!

I can make *you* beautiful!
Yes, even YOU.
No one too old or too ugly.
Only £1 for a new you!!!!!
Hurry!
Special offer ends soon!!!!!!!!!!

Makeovers? *Makeovers?* What an
incredibly stupid idea. Who'd pay to have
a moody old grouch like Margaret smear
gunk all over their face? Ha! No one.

Horrid Henry started laughing and
pointing.

Vain Violet looked like a demon with
red and blue and purple gloop all over
her face. Gorgeous Gurinder looked as if
a paint pot had been poured down her

51

cheeks. Linda's hair looked as if she'd
been struck by lightning.

But Violet wasn't screaming and
yanking Margaret's hair out. Instead she
handed Margaret—*money*.

'Thanks,
Margaret, I look
amazing,' said
Vain Violet,
admiring
herself in the
mirror. Henry
waited for the
mirror to crack.

It didn't.

'Thanks, Margaret,' said Gurinder. 'I look so fantastic I hardly recognise myself.' And she also handed Margaret a pound.

Two whole pounds? Were they mad?

'Are you getting ready for the Monster's Ball?' jeered Henry.

'Shut up, Henry,' said Vain Violet.

'Shut up, Henry,' said Gorgeous Gurinder.

'You're just jealous because I'm going to be rich and you're not,' said Margaret. 'Nah nah ne nah nah.'

'Why don't we give Henry a makeover?' said Violet.

'Good idea,' said Moody Margaret. 'He could sure use one.'

'Yeah,' said Sour Susan.

Horrid Henry took a step back.

Margaret advanced towards him wielding nail varnish and a hairbrush.

Violet followed clutching a lipstick, spray dye and other instruments of torture.

Yikes! Horrid Henry nipped back to the safety of his fort as fast as he could, trying to ignore the horrible, cackling laughter.

He sat on his Purple Hand throne and scoffed some extra tasty chocolate biscuits from the secret stash he'd nicked from Margaret yesterday. Makeovers! Ha! How dumb could you get? Trust a pea-brained grouch like Margaret to come up with such a stupid idea. Who in their right mind would want a makeover?

On the other hand . . .

Horrid Henry had actually seen Margaret being paid. And good money, too, just for smearing some coloured gunk onto people's faces and yanking their hair about.

Hmmmn.

Horrid Henry started to think. Maybe Margaret *did* have a little eensy-weensy teeny-tiny bit of a good idea. And, naturally, anything she could do, Henry could do much, much better. Margaret obviously didn't know the first thing about makeovers, so why should *she* make all that money, thought Horrid Henry indignantly. He'd steal — no, *borrow* — her idea and do it better. Much much better. He'd make people look *really* fantastic.

Henry's Makeovers. Henry's Marvellous Makeovers. Henry's Miraculous Makeovers.

He'd be rich! With some false teeth and red marker he could turn Miss Battle-Axe into a vampire. Mrs Oddbod could be a perfect Dracula. And wouldn't Stuck-Up Steve be improved after a short visit from the Makeover Magician? Even Aunt Ruby wouldn't recognise him when Henry had finished. Tee hee.

First, he needed supplies. That was easy: Mum had tons of gunk for smearing all over her face. And if he ran out he could always use crayons and glue.

Horrid Henry dashed to the bathroom and helped himself to a few handfuls of Mum's makeup. What on earth did she need all this stuff for, thought Henry, piling it into a bag.

About time someone cleared out this drawer. Then he wrote a few leaflets.

Horrid Henry, Makeover Magician, was ready for business.

All he needed were some customers. Preferably rich, ugly customers. Now, where could he find some of those?

Henry strolled into the sitting room. Dad was reading on the sofa. Mum was working at the computer.

Horrid Henry looked at his aged, wrinkly, boring old parents. Bleeeccch!

Boy, could they be improved, thought

Henry. How could he tactfully persuade these potential customers that they needed his help – fast?

'Mum,' said Henry, 'you know Great-Aunt Greta?'

'Yes,' said Mum.

'Well, you're starting to look just like her.'

'What?' said Mum.

'Yup,' said Horrid Henry, 'old and ugly. Except—' he peered at her, 'you have more wrinkles.'

'*What?*' squeaked Mum.

'And Dad looks like a gargoyle,' said Henry.

'Huh?' said Dad.

'Only scarier,' said Henry. 'But don't worry, I can help.'

'Oh really?' said Mum.

'Oh really?' said Dad.

'Yeah,' said Henry, 'I'm doing makeovers.' He handed Mum and Dad a leaflet.

Are you ugly?

Are you very very ugly?

Do you look like the creature from the black lagoon? (Only worse?)

Then today is your lucky day!

HENRY'S
MARVELLOUS MAKEOVERS.

Only £2 for an exciting new you!!!!!!

'So, how many makeovers would you like?' said Horrid Henry. 'Ten? Twenty? Maybe more 'cause you're so old and need a lot of work to fix you.'

'Make over someone else,' said Mum, scowling.

'Make over someone else,' said Dad, scowling.

Boy, talk about ungrateful, thought Horrid Henry.

'Me first!'

'No me!'

Screams were coming from Margaret's garden. Kung-Fu Kate and Singing Soraya were about to become her latest victims. Well, not if Henry could help it.

'Step right up, get your makeovers here!' shouted Henry. 'Miracle Makeovers, from an expert. Only £2 for a brand new you.'

'Leave my customers alone, copycat!'

hissed Moody Margaret, holding out her hand to snatch Kate's pound.

Henry ignored her.

'You look boring, Kate,' said Henry. 'Why don't you let a *real* expert give you a makeover?'

'You?' said Kate.

'Two pounds and you'll look completely different,' said Horrid Henry. 'Guaranteed.'

'Margaret's only charging £1,' said Kate.

'My special offer today is 75p for the

first makeover,' said Henry quickly. 'And free beauty advice,' he added.

Soraya looked up. Kate stood up from Margaret's chair.

'Such as?' scowled Margaret. 'Go on, tell us.'

Eeeek. What on earth *was* a beauty tip? If your face is dirty, wash it? Use a nit comb? Horrid Henry had no idea.

'Well, in your case wear a bag over your head,' said Horrid Henry. 'Or a bucket.'

Susan snickered.

'Ha ha, very funny,' snapped Margaret. 'Come on, Kate. Don't let him trick you. *I'm* the makeover expert.'

'I'm going to try Henry,' said Kate.

'Me too,' said Soraya.

Yippee! His first customers. Henry

stuck out his tongue at Margaret.

Kung-Fu Kate and Singing Soraya climbed over the wall and sat down on the bench at the picnic table. Henry opened his makeover bag and got to work.

'No peeking,' said Henry. 'I want you to be surprised.'

Henry smeared and coated, primped and coloured, slopped and glopped. This was easy!

'I'm so beautiful — hoo hoo hoo,' hummed Soraya.

'Aren't you going to do my hair?' said Kung-Fu Kate.

'Naturally,' said Horrid Henry.

He emptied a pot of glue on her head and scrunched it around.

'What have you put in?' said Kate.

'Secret hair potion,' said Henry.

'What about *me*?' said Soraya.

'No problem,' said Henry, shovelling in some red paint.

A bit of black here, a few blobs of red there, a smear of purple and . . . way hey!

Henry stood back to admire his handiwork. Wow! Kung-Fu Kate looked *completely* different. So did Singing Soraya. Next time he'd charge £10. The moment people saw them everyone would want one of Henry's marvellous makeovers.

'You look amazing,' said Horrid Henry. He had no idea he was such a brilliant makeover artist. Customers would be queueing for his services. He'd need a bigger piggybank.

'There, just like the Mummy,

Frankenstein, *and* a vampire,' said Henry, handing Kate a mirror.

'**AAAARRRRGGGGGHHH!**'

screamed Kung-Fu Kate.

Soraya snatched the mirror.

'**AAAARRRRGGGGGHHH!**'

screamed Singing Soraya.

Horrid Henry stared at them. Honestly, there was no pleasing some people.

'**NOOOooooo**'

squealed Kung-Fu Kate.

'But I thought you wanted to look amazing,' said Henry.

'Amazingly good! Not scary!' wailed Kate.

'Has anyone seen my new lipsticks?' said Mum. 'I could have sworn I put them in the—'

She caught sight of Soraya and Kate.

'AAAAAAARRRRRGGGGGHHHH!'

screeched Mum. 'Henry! How could you be so horrid? Go to your room.'

'But . . . but . . .' gasped Horrid Henry. It was so unfair. Was it his fault his stupid customers didn't know when they looked great?

Henry stomped up the stairs. Then he sighed. Maybe he did need a little more makeover practice before he opened for business.

Now, where could he find someone to practise on?

'I got an A on my spelling test,' said Perfect Peter.

'I got a gold star for having the tidiest drawer,' said Tidy Ted.

'And I got in the Good as Gold book again,' said Goody-Goody Gordon.

Henry burst into Peter's bedroom.

'I'm doing makeovers,' said Horrid Henry. 'Who wants to go first?'

'Uhhmmm,' said Peter.

'Uhhmmm,' said Ted.

'We're going to Sam's birthday party today,' said Gordon.

'Even better,' said Henry beaming. 'I can make you look great for the party. Who's first?'

4

....

HORRiD HENRY'S AUTHOR ViSiT

Horrid Henry woke up. He felt strange. He felt . . . happy. He felt . . . excited. But why?

Was it the weekend? No. Was it a day off school? No. Had Miss Battle-Axe been kidnapped by aliens and transported to another galaxy to slave in the salt mines? No (unfortunately).

So why was he feeling so excited on a school day?

And then Horrid Henry remembered.

Oh wow!! It was Book Week at Henry's school, and his favourite author in the whole world, TJ Fizz, the writer of the stupendous *Ghost Quest* and *Mad Machines* and *Skeleton Skunks* was coming to talk to his class. Henry had read every single one of TJ's brilliant books, even after lights out. Rude Ralph thought they were almost as good as Mutant Max comics. Horrid Henry thought they were even better.

Perfect Peter bounced into his room.

'Isn't it exciting, Henry?' said Perfect Peter. 'Our class is going to meet a real live author! Milksop Miles is coming today. He's the man who wrote *The Happy Nappy*. Do you think he'd sign my copy?'

Horrid Henry snorted.

The Happy Nappy! Only the dumbest book ever. All those giant nappies with names like Rappy Nappy and Zappy Nappy and Tappy Nappy dancing and prancing about. And then the truly

70

horrible Gappy Nappy, who was always wailing, 'I'm leaking!'

Horrid Henry shuddered. He was amazed that Milksop Miles dared to show his face after writing such a boring book.

'Only a wormy toad like you could like such a stupid story,' said Henry.

'It's not stupid,' said Peter.

'Is too.'

'Is not. And he's bringing his guitar. Miss Lovely said so.'

'Big deal,' said Horrid Henry. '*We've* got TJ Fizz.'

71

Perfect Peter shuddered.

'Her books are too scary,' said Peter.

'That's 'cause you're a baby.'

'Mum!' shrieked Peter. 'Henry called me baby.'

'Telltale,' hissed Henry.

'Don't be horrid, Henry,' shouted Mum.

Horrid Henry sat in class with a huge carrier bag filled with all his TJ Fizz books. Everyone in the class had drawn book covers for *Ghost Quest* and *Ghouls' Jewels,* and written their own *Skeleton Skunk* story. Henry's of course was the best: *Skeleton Skunk meets Terminator*

Gladiator: May the smelliest fighter win! He would give it to TJ Fizz if she paid him a million pounds.

Ten minutes to go. How could he live until it was time for her to arrive?

Miss Battle-Axe cleared her throat.

'Class, we have a very important guest coming. I know you're all very excited, but I will not tolerate anything but perfect behaviour today. Anyone who misbehaves will be sent out. Is that clear?' She glared at Henry.

Henry scowled back. Of course he would be perfect. TJ Fizz was coming!

'Has everyone thought of a good question to ask her? I'll write the best ones on the board,' continued Miss Battle-Axe.

'How much money do you make?' shouted Rude Ralph.

'How many TVs do you have?' shouted Horrid Henry.

'Do you like fudge?' shouted Greedy Graham.

'I said *good* questions,' snapped Miss Battle-Axe. 'Bert, what's your question for TJ Fizz?'

'I dunno,' said Beefy Bert.

Rumble.

Rumble.

Rumble.

Ooops. Henry's tummy was telling him it was snacktime.

It must be all the excitement. It was strictly forbidden to eat in class, but Henry was a master sneaker. He certainly wouldn't want his tummy to gurgle while TJ Fizz was talking.

Miss Battle-Axe was writing down Clever Clare's eight questions on the board.

Slowly, carefully, silently, Horrid Henry opened his lunchbox under the table. Slowly, carefully, silently, he eased open the bag of crisps.

Horrid Henry looked to the left.

Rude Ralph was waving his hand in the air.

Horrid Henry looked to the right.

Greedy Graham was drooling and opening a bag of sweets.

The coast was clear. Henry popped some Super Spicy Hedgehog crisps into his mouth.

MUNCH! CRUNCH!

'C'mon Henry, give me some crisps,' whispered Rude Ralph.

'No,' hissed Horrid Henry. 'Eat your own.'

'I'm starving,' moaned Greedy Graham. 'Gimme a crisp.'

'No!' hissed Horrid Henry.

Huh?

Miss Battle-Axe towered over him holding aloft his bag of crisps. Her red eyes were like two icy daggers.

'What did I tell you, Henry?' said Miss Battle-Axe. 'No bad behaviour would be tolerated. Go to Miss Lovely's class.'

'But . . . but . . . TJ Fizz is coming!' spluttered Horrid Henry. 'I was just—'

Miss Battle-Axe pointed to the door. 'Out!'

'NOOOOOOOOOO!' howled Henry.

Horrid Henry sat in a tiny chair at the back of Miss Lovely's room. Never had he suffered such torment. He tried to block his ears as Milksop Miles read his horrible book to Peter's class.

'Hello, Happy, Clappy and Yappy! Can *you* find the leak?'

'No,' said Happy.

'No,' said Clappy.

'No,' said Yappy.

'I can,' said Gappy Nappy.

AAAARRRRGGGGGHHH! Horrid Henry gritted his teeth. He would go mad having to listen to this a moment longer.

He had to get out of here.

'All together now, let's sing the Happy Nappy song,' trilled Milksop Miles, whipping out his guitar.

'Yay!' cheered the infants.

No, groaned Horrid Henry.

Oh I'm a happy nappy,
a happy zappy nappy
I wrap up your bottom, snug and tight,
And keep you dry all through the night
Oh –

This was torture. No, this was worse than torture. How could he sit here listening to the horrible Happy Nappy song knowing that just above him TJ Fizz was reading from one of her incredible books, passing round the famous skunk skeleton, and showing off her *Ghost Quest* drawings. He had to get back to his own class. He had to.

But how?

What if he joined in the singing? He could bellow:

> Oh I'm a soggy nappy
> A smelly, stinky nappy–

Yes! That would certainly get him sent out the door straight to — the head. Not back to his class and TJ Fizz.

Horrid Henry closed his mouth. Rats.

Maybe there'd be an earthquake? A power failure? Where was a fire-drill when you needed one?

He could always pretend he needed the toilet. But then when he didn't come back they'd come looking for him.

Or maybe he could just sneak away? Why not? Henry got to his feet and began to slide towards the door, trying to be invisible.

Sneak Sneak Sn _

'Whooa, come back here, little boy,' shouted Milksop Miles, twanging his guitar. Henry froze. 'Our party is just starting. Now who knows the Happy Nappy dance?'

'I do,' said Perfect Peter.

'I do,' said Goody-Goody Gordon.

'We all do,' said Tidy Ted.

'Everyone on their feet,' said Milksop Miles. 'Ah-one ah-two, let's all do the Nappy Dance!'

'Nap nap nap nap nap nap nappy,' warbled Miles.

'Nap nap nap nap nap nap nappy,' warbled Peter's class, dancing away.

Desperate times call for desperate measures. Horrid Henry started dancing. Slowly, he tapped his way closer and closer and closer to the door and — freedom!

Horrid Henry reached for the door knob. Miss Lovely was busy dancing in the corner. Just a few more steps . . .

'Who's going to be my little helper while we act out the story?' beamed Miles. 'Who would like to play the Happy Nappy?'

'Me! Me!' squealed Miss Lovely's class.

Horrid Henry sank against the wall.

'Come on, don't be shy,' said Miles, pointing straight at Henry. 'Come on up and put on the magic happy nappy!' And he marched over and dangled an enormous blue nappy in front of Henry. It was over one metre wide and one metre high, with a hideous smiling face and big goggly eyes.

Horrid Henry took a step back. He felt faint. The giant nappy was looming above him. In a moment it would be over his head and he'd be trapped inside. His name would be mud — forever. Henry the nappy. Henry the giant nappy. Henry the giant happy nappy . . .

'**AAAARRRRGGGGGHHH!**' screamed Horrid Henry. 'Get away from me!'

Milksop Miles stopped waving the gigantic nappy.

'Oh dear,' he said.

'Oh dear,' said Miss Lovely.

'Don't be scared,' said Miles.

Scared? Horrid Henry . . . scared? Of a giant nappy? Henry opened his mouth to scream.

And then he stopped.

What if . . . ?

'Help! Help! I'm being attacked by a nappy!' screeched Henry. 'HELLLLLLLP!'

Milksop Miles looked at Miss Lovely. Miss Lovely looked at Milksop Miles.

'HELLLLLLLP! HELLLLLLLP!'

'Henry? Are you OK?' piped Perfect Peter.

'NOOOOOOOO!' wailed Horrid Henry, cowering. 'I'm . . . I'm . . . nappy-phobic.'

'Never mind,' said Milksop Miles. 'You're not the first boy who's been scared of a giant nappy.'

'I'm sure I'll be fine if I go back to my

own class,' gasped Horrid Henry.

Miss Lovely hesitated. Horrid Henry opened his mouth to howl —

'Run along then,' said Miss Lovely quickly.

Horrid Henry did not wait to be asked twice.

He raced out of Miss Lovely's class, then dashed upstairs to his own.

Skeleton Skunk here I come, thought Henry, bursting through the door.

There was the great and glorious TJ Fizz, just about to start reading a brand new chapter from her latest book, *Skeleton Stinkbomb*. Hallelujah, he was in time.

'Henry, what are you doing here?' hissed Miss Battle-Axe.

'Miss Lovely sent me back,' beamed Horrid Henry. 'And you did say we should be on our best behaviour today, so I did what I was told.'

Henry sat down as TJ began to read. The story was amazing.

Ahhh, sighed Horrid Henry happily, wasn't life grand?

Visit Horrid Henry's website at **www.horridhenry.co.uk** for competitions, games, downloads and a monthly newsletter!